Limburger's Little White Lie

A Story About Telling the Truth

Featuring the Psalty family of characters
created by Ernie and Debby Rettino

Written by Ken Gire
Illustrated by John Dickenson,
Bob Payne, and Matt Mew

Published by Focus on the Family Publishing/Maranatha! for Kids

P. O. Box 500, Arcadia, CA 91006. Distributed by Word Books, Waco, Texas.

Library of Congress Catalog Card Number 87-81593
ISBN 084-9999-979

On a cold and rainy night, Charity Churchmouse heard a knock on her attic door.

"Knock, knock, knock!" came the rap at the door. "Knock, knock, knock!"

"Coming," responded Charity, in her high voice.

"KNOCK, KNOCK, KNOCK, KNOCK, KNOCK!" The banging grew louder.

"All right," Charity called. "I'm coming, I'm coming!" She opened the door to find three shivering little mice— Mozzarella, Provolone, and Limburger.

"Well, if it isn't the Cheeses for Jesus," said Charity with a warm smile. "Come in, come in. You all look so very cold!"

And faster than the twitch of little mice whiskers, they scampered into Charity's warm home in the attic above the church choir loft.

"Our h-h-heater broke down at our h-h-house," began Mozzarella, her voice shaking and shivering.

"And w-w-we w-w-were w-w-wondering if we might s-s-stay—" chattered the freezing Provolone.

"With ah-ah-ah-AHCHOO!!!" sneezed Limburger, and the force of the sneeze tossed him into a somersault.

"Bless you!" said Charity. "Of course you can stay. Here, come warm yourselves by the fire."

The Cheeses all rushed over to the fireplace and began rubbing their little mice hands and stomping their little mice feet.

"You must be starved," said Charity.

They were still so cold that it hurt to speak. So they all just nodded their heads that, yes, they were very hungry, indeed.

"Very well," Charity said with a smile. "Sit tight, and I'll bring you a nice, hot meal."

The three mice huddled by the fire and slowly started to warm themselves. As they did, drops of water began rolling off the tips of their little mice ears, and kerplopping into big-sized puddles around their little mice feet.

When Charity returned, she brought each mouse a huge plate of hot, steaming vegetables.

"Broccoli?" muttered Mozzarella in surprise.

"Brussels sprouts?" said Provolone, wrinkling up his nose.

"Cauliflower?" Limburger said, raising his eyebrows.

Then, at the same time, they all turned toward Charity. One look at their little mice frowns, and Charity knew something was wrong.

"We were kind of hoping we could maybe have cheeseburgers," said Mozzarella.

"Or grilled cheese sandwiches," Provolone suggested.

"Or pizza," added Limburger.

"Yes, pizza!" the other two mice chimed in. "Pizza! Pizza! Pizza!"

"I'm sorry, I don't have any pizza," said Charity. "But I've got plenty of vegetables, and they are so-o-o good for you."

When she said this, the mice looked down at their plates. The vegetables just stared back in a healthy sort of way that wasn't at all interesting.

"Do we have to eat this, Charity?" asked Provolone as he pouted.

"Absolutely," Charity said. "I want you to clean your plates."

The mice just sat there, thinking pizza thoughts, but smelling vegetable smells.

"Now, now," said Charity. "I'll go downstairs and bake some big, luscious brownies for dessert. If you eat all your vegetables, you can each have several brownies."

"My stomach still says pizza," said Mozzarella after Charity disappeared downstairs.

"Mine, too," echoed Provolone.

Then Limburger spotted a telephone. "I've got an idea! Let's call out for pizza!"

"You mean...call a pizza place to have it delivered here?" asked Mozzarella.

"Exactly!"

"Great idea, Lim! Great idea!" exclaimed Provolone.

So Limburger dialed the restaurant and ordered a giant-sized pizza with all their favorite toppings—sausage, pineapple, Canadian bacon, and of course, all their favorite cheeses, Mozzarella, Provolone, and Limburger.

When the pizza finally came, they ate as fast as they could. They knew, of course, that Charity could walk through the door at any moment. So they wasted no time talking and just chewed faster and faster and faster with their little mice teeth.

When they finished, they wiped their mouths, leaned back in their chairs, and patted their fat tummies.

"Yummy, yummy, yummy, I've got pizza in my tummy!" said Mozzarella.

"It sure beats vegetables!" Provolone agreed.

"This is really living," said Limburger, propping his feet on the table.

Suddenly they heard Charity's footsteps on the stairs.

"She's coming!" Mozzarella whispered with alarm.

Provolone was so startled that he and his chair fell back with a crash.

"Quick, hide the pizza box!" ordered Limburger. They shoved it under the bed.

"Now, let's get rid of the vegetables," he said.

Mozzarella and Provolone looked at each other nervously. They quickly searched the room for a spot to stuff the vegetables, but they couldn't find any good hiding places.

Then Limburger saw some pipes that rose from the floor toward the ceiling.

"Quick, dump the vegetables down the pipes!" he ordered.

So they all scurried to scrape their plates into the large pipes.

The three mice scampered back to their chairs just as the door opened.

''Fresh luscious brownies!'' Charity announced happily as she entered the room.

''Oh, boy!'' replied the mice as they licked their little mice lips. ''Yum!'' they said as they rubbed their little mice hands.

''Did you eat all your vegetables?'' asked Charity, setting the brownies on the table.

Suddenly the room got very quiet, because the Cheeses for Jesus did not know what to say. Mozzarella and Provolone glanced over at Limburger for help. But the question was so tricky that Limburger felt a twitch in his little mouse nose.

''Well?'' asked Charity. ''Did you or did you not eat all your vegetables?''

A sudden smile spread over Limburger's little mouse face, and he held up his empty dish. ''We cleaned our plates!'' he said loudly, trying not to sound nervous.

''Good job!'' Charity said. ''I'm so proud of you three.''

''We're absolutely, positively stuffed,'' continued Limburger, sounding a little bolder. ''But we saved enough room for brownies!''

When they had finished their dessert, Charity said, "Why don't we all go downstairs, and I'll play a few songs on our new pipe organ."

"Pipe organ?" the mice said together, glancing first at each other and then at the pipes on the other side of the room.

"Uh...maybe we could just sing," Mozzarella said.

"Good idea!" chimed in Provolone.

"Yes, let's sing," Limburger echoed.

But Charity would not take no for an answer and shooed them all downstairs to hear her play.

As the Cheeses for Jesus sat in a pew, Charity began playing the organ. The music was beautiful, but every so often she hit some notes that sounded kind of mushy and squishy.

The Cheeses began to squirm in the pew.

The more Charity played, the more excited she became. The more excited she became, the harder she pushed down on the keys. But when she pushed hard, vegetables started shooting out of the pipes. Boom! Blam! Kaboom!

As everyone sat there, it rained broccoli, brussels sprouts, and cauliflower all over the place. Vegetables splattered against the pulpit, bounced off the pews, and even landed in the offering plate!

The three mice slid off the pew and tried to sneak out the door.

"Wait just one minute!" hollared Charity. The mice froze in their tracks.

"Turn around!" she ordered, and they all turned around.

"Come here!" she commanded, and they all inched forward very, very slowly.

"Now, about those vegetables you told me you ate," Charity began as she squinted at the group of trembling mice. "What do you have to say for yourselves?"

Mozzarella and Provolone nudged Limburger, trying to get him to speak.

"Well?" said Charity, standing there with her hands on her hips.

"I...I...I lied," stammered Limburger. "We did clean our plates. But we didn't eat the vegetables. We just scraped them into the pipes upstairs. It was a mistake, honest! We didn't know they were organ pipes."

"It is sometimes hard to tell the truth," Charity admitted. "But we can do it with God's help. There is a prayer in the Bible that says, 'Oh, God . . . help me to never tell a lie.' The truth is very important to God. In fact, Jesus once said, 'I came to bring truth to the world. All who love the truth are my followers.' "

"But it was just a little white lie," Limburger said, looking down at the floor. "I didn't mean to do any harm."

"You may not have meant any harm, Limburger. But just look around," Charity said gently. "You can see that even a little white lie can make a big mess of things."

Limburger and his friends knew she was right. After all, they were up to their little mice toes in broccoli, brussels sprouts, and cauliflower.

Cleaning up the mess was a squishy, icky job that took a long time. But it was time which Limburger and the other Cheeses for Jesus spent thinking about what they had done.

Limburger felt especially bad since the whole idea had been his. He reached down to pick up one of the last pieces of mushy vegetables. As he tossed it—KERPLOP—into a garbage bag, he decided he would try to never tell a lie again. Even a little white one.